Dry Air and Good Hope

A Story of Early Tombstone

Dry Air and Good Hope

A Story of Early Tombstone

Edith Clairmont

ISBN 978-1-939345-29-5
Library of Congress Control Number: 2026937093

First edition
April, 2026

Published by
Goose Flats Graphics & Publishing
P.O. Box 813
Tombstone, Arizona 85638
(520) 457-3884
gooseflats.com

Book layout & cover design:
Keith Davis
Goose Flats Graphics
Tombstone, Arizona

DEDICATION

To everyone who has ever gone West in search of breath, light, or a place to begin again.

"Home is the nicest word there is."

Laura Ingalls Wilder

"Live in each season as it passes; breathe the air, drink the drink, taste the fruit."

Henry David Thoreau

TABLE of CONTENTS

Chapter 1
Into Thin Air

Arrival in the Desert

The dust found them first. It sifted through the stage curtains and scalloped along the floorboards like pale water, and Eliza Harper—who had crossed the whole wide map looking for air she could swallow without a fight—drew it in and smiled anyway. It was dry, yes, but it did not cling to her ribs the way Ohio's damp had done. The sky outside looked ironed flat, a hard blue handkerchief stretched from one mountain fence to the other.

Nate tipped his hat at the driver and climbed down, then turned to offer his hand. "Careful of the step, Liza." She took it, not because she needed it but because it pleased him to give it, and together they stood blinking on the edge of Allen Street, where the world rattled and clanged like a pocketful of nails. Hammers measured out a steady beat somewhere close; a piano down the way gambled with a melody and lost. Sunlight caught on glass and brass and the nickel shine of a new pump handle at a corner trough.

"Smells like work," Nate said, which was his way of saying it smelled like hope.

They had come by rail to Benson, then by stage over

miles that looked empty until you stared—then they filled with thorn and feather, with shadows that belonged to neither cloud nor man. Tombstone's name had been a dare on a prospector's tongue; now the dare had turned into streets and storefronts, and an appetite for nails and timber big enough to feed a carpenter for years.

Eliza pressed a handkerchief to her lips. Habit. The breath came soft and even. There was a heat in it, yes, but it did not carry the old heaviness; it did not groan at the bottom of her chest the way Februarys in Circleville had taught it to do. She tucked away the cloth and shaded her eyes to read signs—Boarding, Millinery, Hardware, Photograph Gallery, a newspaper office farther along with a painted door that simply said Epitaph.

"Nate," she said, touching his sleeve. "There's a paper."

"Better still, there's a roof over our heads to be found before sundown," he said, but he followed her gaze and smiled. "We'll see it after we stow our earthly goods, Miss Ohio."

Mrs. Boyle's House

Their earthly goods amounted to two trunks, a carpetbag that refused to hold its shape, Nate's saws and planes in a wooden case, and a folded letter from Dr. Bennett of Cincinnati—the one who had said Arizona would give Eliza a fighting chance. The driver hauled the trunks to the boardwalk and tipped his hat toward a sign that read Rooms & Meals—Mrs. T. Boyle, Fair Rates.

"Best hash on the block," he said. "And the lady runs a clean hallway. Watch the second step—she means it."

The second step had a warp that sang underfoot; Nate tested it, squinted, and made a note in his head of shims and nails. The front parlor smelled faintly of soap and strongly of coffee. A woman in a lavender dress that had once been grand, and still was if you squinted, looked up from a ledger with the air of a magistrate weighing sentences.

“You'll be the Harpers,” she said, before either of them spoke. “You look road-dry and honest. Temperance Boyle. Welcome to my temple of peace. If you are not peaceful, you will be. I have ways.” Her eyes softened. “You're the ones from Ohio, the lady with the lungs. Doctor Bennett wired ahead. You'll want the back room—it's cooler by two degrees and looks out on a patch of yard I call a garden because I am an optimist.”

“Mrs. Boyle,” Eliza said, the name tasting kindly in her mouth. “We're much obliged.”

“Obliged comes with supper at six,” Mrs. Boyle replied. “My rates are fair and my coffee is strong and the second step complains. You'll learn its song.”

They signed the ledger. Nate carried their trunks down a corridor that smelled of starch and sun. The back room was narrow and neat and bright. A white bedspread waited like snow. Eliza touched the sill: the wood was cool, the glass warm. To the east, beyond roofs and street, the sky tilted up into a pale brightness. Horizon like a promise. For a moment she only breathed—testing the air the way a swimmer tests water with one foot, surprised and grateful that it held her.

“Wash,” Nate said gently. “Then see about work.”

They scrubbed road grit from their faces and hands at the small basin, smoothed their travel-wrinkled clothes, and stepped back onto Allen Street with Mrs. Boyle's directions folded into Eliza's glove. "Hardware is two doors down from a man who plays the piano in a way that makes me question Providence. The paper is four further; Clara Finch runs the back room there and knows more about commas than the Almighty intends one woman to know."

The Epitaph

The Epitaph kept its door propped open with a stack of old proofs. Inside, the air held a kinship of ink and metal, of paper rubbed soft along the edges. The room hummed with small order—type in their little wooden homes, galleys stacked like obedient soldiers, a composing stone that looked like it knew more secrets than it would ever tell.

A man at a desk peered over spectacles and then past them, toward the street, as if reading an invisible headline. "Subscribers?" he asked.

"Neighbors," Eliza said. "If we behave. I know my way around a frame and chase and pica measure. My father ran a small weekly in Circleville. I can proof names clean and keep a galley from tripping."

The man's mouth tucked itself into a half-smile. "You pitch that like a newsboy. I'm Amos Dake. We can always use eyes that don't fall asleep over the mayor's minutes. Clara!"

From a back corner, footsteps—light, sure—answered the summons. Eliza felt her breath steady further, as if the room's neat rows and honest ink were a kind of medicine.

Chapter 2
The Town Too Tough to Die

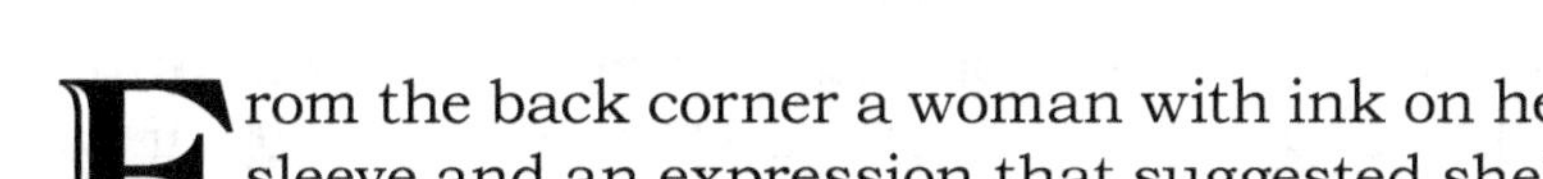

From the back corner a woman with ink on her sleeve and an expression that suggested she'd been born with a composing stick in her hand stepped forward. She had the hands of a person who measured twice, who liked to put the world in order letter by letter.

"You'll be Eliza Harper," she said. "Doctor Avery wrote a neat page and a half about your lungs and your virtues, and I'm prepared to forgive both. We have proofs at four and a schedule that respects fresh air. Can you read bad handwriting kindly?"

"Kindly and aloud," Eliza said. "So even the writer blushes."

Clara looked at Amos. "Do you hear the way she lines up her sentences? We'll make room."

They spoke of hours—modest to begin, mornings when the day was cool—and of pay, which was not grand but honest. Eliza took a breath that reached down without scraping. "I can start tomorrow."

Outside, the sun had moved a finger-width west; shadows curled under porches. Nate had been counting storefronts. "There's a man fitting glass two doors over with a jamb out of true," he said. "And a hardware seller who just asked if I could read a square from across the room. I told him I could read it from Ohio."

"What did he say?" Eliza asked.

"He said come back at seven before the street wakes up and we'll talk wood," Nate replied, pleased. "He's got a back room of planks that look like they want to be useful."

They returned to Mrs. Boyle's with the day's first small promises tucked into their pockets. Supper gathered at six as foretold: stew that sold itself with aroma, biscuits that drew sighs from men who didn't know they were sighing, coffee strong enough to float a spoon. A fiddler named Jasper Corcoran—Jazz to friends, which appeared to be everyone—tucked himself near the sideboard and tried to convince a tune it wanted to be a waltz. Between mouthfuls, the table traded news like chips: pumps thudding below ground, a calf born behind the livery, a photograph man who could make you look honest or guilty with the same trick of light.

"Best mind your tempers," said a soft voice from the end of the table. "Town's still finding its manners." The speaker wore a deputy's star like he regretted the shiny. "Frank Valdez," he added, tipping his head toward the Harpers. "Welcome. Keep your heads level and your feet under you. If heat finds your lungs, come by Dr. Avery's in the morning; he's got a yard with shade that seems to argue with the sun and sometimes wins."

Eliza nodded. "We have his letter," she said. "It got us here."

“That letter has pulled more souls west than the promise of wages,” Mrs. Boyle sniffed. “I’ll not argue with a doctor who can write a sentence that makes a woman breathe freer.”

After, the boarding house settled under the slow drawl of evening. Nate opened their window to invite whatever breeze might be passing by on its way to Mexico. Eliza unfolded a small notebook and listed the day’s mercies: a cool glass of water; a clerk who said ma’am like it meant something; the way the light turned Allen Street’s dust to gold just before supper. She paused, listening to her own chest, the way the breath moved around and did not scrape or complain. She wrote breath light as a ribbon and then scratched it out for sounding too proud.

Night Trouble

Sometime in the deeps of night, when distant boots had gone quiet and even the piano had given up its quarrel with itself, Eliza woke coughing. It was not the old terrible grip, not the cough that spilled heat into her bones, but it shook her and made her eyes water and her chest feel like a knotted sheet. Nate was up at once, fumbling for the lamp, his face turned the way a carpenter turns to a beam he means to set straight.

“I’ll fetch Dr. Avery,” he said. “I can find the street in the dark.”

She caught his sleeve. “It’s passing,” she tried, but the breath bucked again, and for a moment Ohio came back—the wet and the heavy and the way windows sweated in winter like men.

Nate kissed her forehead. “Two streets over. I’ll be faster than common sense.” He thrust bare feet into his boots and had the door half open when a knock landed on the other side of it—quick, polite, as if the night itself had found manners.

Nate drew back and lifted the latch. The hall smelled of soap and cool wood. On the threshold stood a man with his hat in his hands, his coat dusty with the day that had already ended. He had the kind of face that had listened a long time to other people's trouble.

"Mr. Harper," he said in a voice that came folded in blankets, soft and steady. "Frank Valdez. Mrs. Boyle woke me. She said the night took your wife by the throat. I thought to walk you as far as the doctor's, or fetch him if you'd rather stay."

Behind Nate, Eliza's breath drew and snagged and eased. The lamplight made a small sun on the floorboards. Outside, a coyote called like a hinge that wanted oil.

Nate looked once at Eliza and then back at the deputy. "Come in," he said. "Or—no. Help me get him here. If you know the way faster than I can learn it, we'll borrow your feet."

Valdez settled his hat on his head again, efficient as a buckle. "I know the boards that don't squeak," he said, and the two men stepped into the hallway and into the night, which had paused, curious, to see how this new story might want to go.

Chapter 3
Boarding-House Manners

A Morning in Motion

Tombstone woke like a rooster who'd overslept—late, loud, and full of opinions. First came the clatter of a wagon on Allen Street, then the hiss of a cookstove, then the fiddle of Jasper "Jazz" Corcoran teasing a hymn into a dance tune.

Eliza stirred beneath the thin quilt, breathing deep. For the first time in years, the morning air met her lungs without protest. She smiled at the small miracle, then coughed once—more habit than harm.

Nate was already at the basin, sluicing his face with water that smelled faintly of tin. "Doctor Avery promised two things," he said, toweling off. "Dry air and good work. Looks like we've got the first in hand. Today I'll see about the second."

"And I," Eliza said, smoothing her hair, "will see about the Epitaph. Clara Finch said proofs at four. I mean to prove myself before then."

Breakfast at Mrs. Boyle's

Mrs. Temperance Boyle ran her boarding house as though it were both court and classroom. She presided from the head of the table, coffee pot in one hand, judgment in the other.

"This is not a saloon," she warned between servings of bacon. "Voices low, elbows narrow, and gossip only if it serves digestion."

Eliza, seated between Nate and a dressmaker named Maggie O'Rourke, caught Mrs. Boyle's wink and realized the rules were half show, half mercy.

Maggie leaned close. "Don't fret her bark, missus. She feeds us like kings. Only asks that we wipe our boots and remember she was once young and beautiful—and intends we don't forget it."

Nate chuckled, earning a glare from Mrs. Boyle that could have leveled a mule. He wisely applied himself to his biscuit.

Halfway through the meal, Deputy Frank Valdez appeared in the doorway, hat in hand. His voice was mild as dust settling. "Morning, folks. Just a word to our new neighbors—Mr. and Mrs. Harper, isn't it? Allen Street can be lively. Keep your heads level and your tempers cooler. Steel flies quicker than sense in these parts."

Eliza inclined her head. "Thank you, Deputy. I've lived among quarrelsome hens before."

Valdez smiled faintly. "Hens rarely carry Colts. Still, the principle holds."

Nate's Day in Timber

By midmorning, Nate had found work. The hardware man put him on a storefront repair along Fremont where the corner had sagged, the desert tugging it down. Nate crouched, tapped the warped frame, and nodded. “A man’s pride is only as square as his door,” he said, setting to work.

By noon his collar was white with salt, his palms full of splinters—but his spirit lightened with every swing of the hammer. Other tradesmen passed, nodding as if to say, You’ve earned your dust. It was a wordless welcome.

When the proprietor pressed two silver dollars into his hand, Nate turned the coins over slowly, feeling their weight. “Plenty more doors in this town,” the man said. “And windows, and stairs. She’s growing fast.”

Eliza Among the Letters

At the Epitaph, Eliza’s heart thudded faster than her boots. Clara Finch greeted her with a stack of proofs. “Names, dates, places. Don’t let us bury a man in Bisbee who’s still walking Allen Street.”

Eliza bent to the task. She corrected “Cochise” where it had been set as “Coaches,” restored the lost “l” to “Schieffelin,” and tamed a rogue comma or two. Clara glanced over once, then nodded approval—a small miracle in itself.

By four o’clock Eliza’s fingers were ink-stained, her lungs untroubled. When Amos Dake, the editor, looked over her shoulder, he grinned. “Sharp eye, Mrs. Harper. Stay on tomorrow. Tombstone can use a proofreader who doesn’t nod at the devil’s spelling.”

Eliza blushed, unsure whether from pride or heat.

Evening Trials

Supper was stew again—“an entirely different beast from yesterday’s,” Mrs. Boyle claimed. Jazz Corcoran played softly while Maggie O'Rourke told of a runaway mule that flattened her dress stand, and the room rippled with laughter.

But the laughter died when a deep rumble rolled beneath the floorboards. The chandelier swayed; spoons clinked against bowls.

"Mines settling," muttered a miner near the end. "Water pushing where it's got no business."

Eliza caught Nate's sleeve. The shaking faded, but unease lingered like a held breath.

Mrs. Boyle rapped her spoon against the table. "Eat," she ordered. "The world hasn't ended yet, and I'll not have stew wasted on fretting."

Later, in their room, Eliza scribbled in her notebook before sleep claimed her: The ground itself seems to whisper—remember where you've come.

~~~

The boarding house settled into quiet breaths. Nate dreamed of timber holding firm against unseen weight. Eliza dreamed of letters marching into clean columns.

But somewhere below, past rock and rib and all the brave faces of men, the water pressed closer. And Tombstone—bright, brash, unbowed—pretended not to hear.
~~~

Chapter 4
The Weight of Timber

The desert morning was cool enough to make a man believe in mercy. Nate Harper strode toward the Grand Central Mine with a lunch pail Mrs. Boyle had packed—bread, cheese, and an apple that cost more than a hammer handle. Beside him walked two other hires, both older, both quiet in that way men are when they measure a newcomer.

At the mouth of the shaft, Silas P. Kittredge waited, a man of angles and rules. His spectacles pinched his nose; his boots bore more polish than most engineers dared in the field. "You'll be timbermen today," he said. "Which means you'll keep the roof above us and the sides from kissing each other. No work, no breath. Simple as that."

Nate nodded. He knew timber—Ohio barns, schoolhouses, pews—but never timber meant to stand between a man and the weight of the world.

Down in the Dark

The cage dropped like a swallowed stone, air growing damp and sharp with mineral scent. Nate gripped the chain and felt his stomach rise. Lamps below made a faint yellow promise in the black.

They stepped into a gallery where walls sweated and timbers stood like ribs. Water dripped steady as a clock. Men swung picks in rhythm, their breaths clouding lamp smoke.

Kittredge led them to a sagging stretch. "Cut braces and set 'em quick. Wedge, tap, test. Listen for the groan. The mine tells you when it's content."

Nate set his saw to pine, heart steadying with each stroke. Wood chips fell on rock like confetti from another world. He shaped the brace, set it, and tapped with a mallet. The timber pressed against stone, and for a moment the weight of mountains argued with his arm—then settled. Silence followed. A silence that meant safety.

Eliza's Walk

Aboveground, Eliza followed one of Dr. Avery's prescribed "breathing walks." She wandered east along Fremont until the town thinned into scrub brush and dry washes. The air here was a clean blade, cutting away the heaviness that had once pinned her chest.

She paused at a rise, noting the scatter of rooftops, the curls of stove smoke, the clatter that marked Tombstone as alive. In her notebook she wrote: Allen Street runs like a fiddle tune—fast, bright, and off-key. Fremont hums steadier, like a hymn. Between them lies our chance.

When she returned, Clara Finch stood by the Epitaph door, waving a sheet. "Proofs are late, Mrs. Harper. Seems the town breathes no easier than you."

Eliza laughed, a sound that carried without strain.

The Cave-In

Below, Nate's hammer struck—and then, too quick for thought, the gallery shuddered. A blast misfired in the next drift, the concussion ripping through stone. The nearest lamp snuffed, plunging them into dark.

Men shouted. Rock cracked. The air filled with choking dust. Nate dropped to his knees, groping for the brace he'd just set. It held. But another down the line groaned like a dying ox.

"Light!" someone cried. "Bring the lamp!"

A faint flame licked back to life, showing a man pinned by a slab, his leg caught. Nate scrambled, heart pounding. He wedged his shoulder against the stone, straining. The timber above moaned, then steadied. Other hands joined his—calloused, desperate. Together they levered the man free. He screamed, then breathed—and that breath sounded louder than the mine itself.

Kittredge's face appeared through the haze, pale but composed. "Out," he ordered. "We clear until the ground forgives us."

Nate staggered into the cage, arms trembling, chest burning with dust. The rescued miner leaned on him, muttering thanks through clenched teeth. When daylight struck their faces, it felt like being reborn.

Supper and Silence

That night at Mrs. Boyle's, the table buzzed with talk of the cave-in. Everyone knew before Nate sat down—news traveled faster than bullets in Tombstone.

"You pulled McGinnis out," Jazz Corcoran said, bow balanced on his knee. "Word is he owes you both legs and a fiddle tune."

Nate shook his head. "It was more hands than mine. Timber held, else we'd all be swallowed."

Eliza's hand found his under the table, cool and steady. She looked at him with pride and something deeper—fear, perhaps, of how close he'd come to being buried with strangers.

Mrs. Boyle poured coffee. "This town eats men like stew," she said. "You've had your first taste. Don't offer it seconds."

The chandelier above swayed gently, though no tremor came this time.

Eliza's Notes

Later, while Nate slept with his arm flung over his brow, Eliza wrote: Today the earth reminded us it has more say than men with picks. But timber, true and firm, can argue back. Nate set a brace, and the brace held, and because of it a man breathes still. This town is stitched together with sweat and stubbornness. I begin to think we may belong here after all.

She listened to the boarding house breathe—creaks, snores, a distant fiddle tuning itself against silence. Beneath it all, she fancied she could hear the pumps of the mine far below, beating like another heart for Tombstone.

At dawn, Nate stirred, murmuring in his sleep, "Set, wedge, tap, breathe." Eliza smiled into the dim light. The mine's rhythm had entered his dreams—perhaps their lives as well.

Chapter 5
Ink & Breath

The Morning Breathes

The morning light spilled pale and clean across the boarding-house curtains. Eliza woke with the curious calm that came only when her chest allowed it. She tested a deep breath—no scrape, no catch—and smiled. Nate was already at the basin, sleeves rolled, water shining on his wrists.

"You've got color," he said, surprised, almost reverent.

"Perhaps Tombstone is keeping its promise," Eliza replied. She tied her hair back and reached for her shawl. "Clara will want me early at the Epitaph. I must not keep her waiting."

Mrs. Boyle fortified them with biscuits wrapped in cloth and her usual commandments. "Stay on the shady side till noon, don't argue with men who drink before breakfast, and keep your boots polished. This town may be rough, but there's no call to look it."

Nate grinned. "She runs us like soldiers."

"And keeps us alive like one," Eliza said.

At the Epitaph

The Epitaph rattled with type. Amos Dake scowled over his desk, muttering about patent-medicine men with grievances. Clara Finch emerged from the back, a sheaf of proofs in hand.

"Here," she said briskly. "Names, dates, places. Catch them before they embarrass us."

Eliza bent over the galley, correcting "Safford" where it had been set "Saffrod," restoring a missing "l" to Schieffelin, straightening a crooked column. Her pencil worked steadily, each correction a small defense against chaos.

By midday, her fingertips were smudged with ink but her lungs still steady. Clara set down her stick. "That's enough. Dr. Avery says you're to walk. Bring back the color of the light—we'll tuck it into that little column of yours."

Dr. Avery's Yard

Eliza found Dr. Avery watering a young cottonwood. His sleeves were rolled, his manner patient. "Mrs. Harper," he said. "Tell me truly: how are you breathing?"

"Like a woman who has remembered she owns her lungs," she answered.

He smiled. "Then keep them obedient. In four counts, hold two, out slow. Don't gallop your strength to impress the neighbors."

They paced the small yard together. The shade from the cottonwood was thin, but she felt it as a benediction. She returned to town with her notebook open, jotting: The air here is thin but honest, and that counts as kindness.

Nate's News

She met Nate coming up Fremont, shirt damp with sweat, sawdust in his hair. "The hardware man signed me for the week," he said, pleased. "And Kittredge wants me again tomorrow. Looks like Tombstone means to feed us."

She kissed the back of his scraped hand. "We'll eat well on honesty and biscuits."

By late afternoon she was back at the Epitaph. Amos waved an editorial: Bottled Thunder and Other Deceptions. It skewered miracle cures with a sharp pen. Eliza proofed it carefully, catching a misprint that would have turned "peddlers" into "peddlars."

At the bottom of another galley, in type small as sparrow tracks, appeared her own words—Notes on the Sunrise Walk. Only inches of space, but enough to make her heart flutter.

Shadows in the Street

At supper Mrs. Boyle served roast chicken while Jazz Corcoran fiddled soft tunes. Nate was still at the mine, leaving Eliza between Maggie O'Rourke and Clara. When the meal ended, she wrapped her shawl tight and stepped out into the evening alone.

Allen Street blazed with laughter and cards. Near the corner a man in a fine hat stood atop a crate, bottles of amethyst glass gleaming beside him. His voice carried smooth as oil.

"Ladies and gentlemen, I bring you Dr. Bliss's Pulmonary Lightning—cures coughs, sweetens breath, scours lungs!"

His eyes found Eliza, shawl drawn close. "You there, madam—from Ohio, I'll wager? This will send your cough packing."

Eliza lifted her chin and passed him, ignoring the laughter that followed. By the time she reached Fremont the boardwalk had thinned. Footsteps echoed behind—steady, deliberate. She lengthened her stride, then remembered Avery's lesson: calm is stronger than fear.

A shadow detached from a doorway and matched her pace. At the Epitaph corner Clara Finch appeared, taking her arm. "Walk with me," she said, too evenly. Together they climbed Mrs. Boyle's steps. Across the street the salesman lingered, bottle in hand, smile practiced and cold.

"Evening, Mrs. Harper," he said softly. "You and your editor grew mighty free with words today. We'll have to speak on what's fair." He tipped his hat, then melted into the dusk.

~~~

Mrs. Boyle's silhouette filled the doorway, apron tied like a banner of war. Eliza slipped inside, her breath steady but heavy, as if the town had leaned down to test her resolve. Tombstone had given her air, yes—but also its first warning.
~~~

Chapter 6
A Lesson in the Street

The following morning brought warmth quick and fierce. By the time Mrs. Boyle's table cleared, Allen Street already rang with hammer blows and the laughter of men who had worked too little and drank too much. Eliza, shawl at her shoulders, slipped toward the Epitaph, determined to forget the salesman's shadow from the night before.

Clara greeted her with brisk composure and a pile of proofs. "Names, Mrs. Harper. Keep them honest. If we bury the wrong man again, his widow may sue us for libel." The familiar task steadied Eliza. She bent over the galleys, letting the rhythm of letters and commas restore calm.

By noon the presses rumbled to life. Amos Dake leaned in the doorway, eyes on the street. "Town's humming too loud today," he muttered. "Trouble smells like whiskey before breakfast."

Nate's Day

Down at the Grand Central shaft, Nate set braces against the groaning rock. The work was steady, but his mind kept straying upward, wondering how Eliza fared with her own trials. When the shift ended early—

Kittredge needing a pump repaired—Nate washed his face and walked Allen Street with purpose.

Near the mercantile he found Eliza stepping out, papers in hand. She smiled, but her eyes flicked warily to the corners.

“I’m fine,” she said before he asked. “Clara walked me partway.”

“You’ll not walk alone when the sun drops,” Nate said. “I’ll see to it.”

The Street Showdown

That promise was tested sooner than either wished.

Late that afternoon the amethyst-bottle salesman reappeared, his crate perched near the Occidental. His voice carried oily and loud, mocking the editorial that had cut into his business.

“This so-called paper accuses honest men!” he cried. “Names no names, but points crooked fingers! They say I’m a fraud—yet look! One sip and I’ll show you lungs like bellows!”

The crowd jeered and laughed. Then his eyes found Eliza again. “There’s the lady herself! The proofreader! Ask her if I lie!”

Eliza froze, heat rising in her cheeks. Before she could answer, Deputy Frank Valdez stepped from the boardwalk’s edge, voice calm as dust. “That’s enough, Carrow. Take your tonic and move along.”

The salesman sneered. “You protect liars, Deputy? This woman sharpens the editor’s knife.”

Valdez’s hand brushed his belt—but Nate moved quicker. He stepped between Eliza and the crate, his stance plain and steady. "She owes you nothing," he said. "Best pack your bottles before they spill."

For a breath, the crowd hushed. Then Carrow spat into the dirt. "This town will choke on its pride," he muttered, gathering his bottles. He vanished down the alley, curses following him like flies.

Valdez watched until the street settled again. "Be careful," he said quietly. "Some men can't abide being corrected in print."

Evening Calm

That night at Mrs. Boyle's, the boarding house felt warmer, safer. Maggie O'Rourke insisted on sewing Eliza a lighter dress "to keep Tombstone from thinking you're made of Ohio frost," and Jazz Corcoran struck up a reel until even Mrs. Boyle's stern face softened.

Later, in their room, Nate brushed a thumb along Eliza's cheek. "This town tests us," he said.

"But we'll answer together," she replied.

"Tombstone may roar," she added softly, "but it hasn't chased me yet."

Outside, the wind moved through mesquite, carrying laughter, hammer blows, and the faint rattle of bottles—like a warning that hadn't quite given up.

Chapter 7
Schieffelin Waltz

A Promise of Music

Summer heat pressed hard upon Tombstone, but the promise of music softened the evening. Word spread that a concert would be held at Schieffelin Hall, and Mrs. Boyle pressed tickets into her boarders' hands.

"Culture," she declared, "is the only thing that keeps a mining camp from gnawing on itself. You will go, clap politely, and keep stew off your Sunday clothes."

Eliza hesitated. "I'm not certain I can stand through it."

"You'll sit," Nate replied. "And if you cough, I'll clap louder to cover it." His grin won her over.

Schieffelin Hall

The evening light was warm as honey when they joined the crowd filing into the hall. The building stood proud on Fremont, adobe walls and tall, narrow, double-hung sash windows lending dignity to a rough town. Lamps glowed across rows of polished benches, and the air buzzed with chatter—merchants, miners, wives, and children united in anticipation.

Jazz Corcoran tuned his fiddle at the stage's edge, nodding to Nate and Eliza like honored guests. Clara Finch sat two rows ahead, notebook ready to review every note. Even Deputy Valdez leaned against the wall, faintly amused.

When the music began, the hall transformed. Fiddles, piano, and cornet carried waltzes and reels, melodies both lively and sweet. Eliza found herself swaying without thought, her hand in Nate's. For a time, her breath followed the rhythm instead of fighting it. She even stood for a piece, letting the tune guide a slow, careful step.

"You're lighter on your feet than you claim," Nate murmured.

"And you're heavier than you admit," she shot back, laughing.

Fire on Fremont

Joy in Tombstone rarely lingers. Near the end of the evening, as applause rang out, the smell of smoke crept through the hall. A shout carried from outside—"Fire at the livery!"

The crowd broke like water. People rushed into the night, skirts lifted, hats pressed tight. From Fremont they saw flames clawing skyward at the edge of Allen Street, sparks threatening rooftops.

Nate thrust Eliza's hand toward Clara. "Stay with her!" he called, then joined the bucket line forming at the pump. Men passed brimming pails hand to hand, women doused rooftops to keep sparks from finding a meal.

Eliza stood with Clara at the edge, her chest tight but her eyes steady. She watched Nate haul water until his shirt clung dark and his arms shook. She longed to run to him, but Clara's grip held firm. "He'll stand straighter knowing you're watching," Clara said.

Hours passed—shouts, splashes, and the hiss of steam marking the fight. When the roof collapsed in sparks and smoke, the blaze gave up. The bucket line slowed, then stopped. Tombstone stood—scorched, singed, but unbroken.

After the Flames

Nate stumbled back to Eliza, coughing black smoke, his face streaked with ash. She caught his arm. "You fool," she whispered, though her eyes were wet.

"Better a fool than a coward," he rasped.

Mrs. Boyle appeared, apron singed, hair escaping its pins. "Everyone back to the boarding house," she barked. "I've stew enough for an army, and you'll wash before you sit on my chairs."

That night, the boarders gathered—sooty, weary, but alive. Jazz coaxed a soft tune from his fiddle while men and women spoke of narrow escapes. Eliza held Nate's hand beneath the table, proud, fearful, and certain that this town demanded more courage than most.

Later, she wrote: Tonight I learned how quickly joy can catch fire, and how neighbors pass water hand to hand until they feel like family. Tombstone may burn, but it does not surrender.

She closed the book, listening to the hush after so much noise. Nate's breath evened into sleep beside her. From the street outside came the faintest note of a fiddle, still playing as though music might keep the embers from rising again.

Chapter 8
Smoke Signals

Morning came with the smell of damp ashes. Allen Street bore the marks of the fire—charred beams, scorched shingles, buckets scattered like tired soldiers. Yet the town buzzed with pride rather than despair.

"Could've lost half the block," men said at the pumps. "Lucky we stopped it where we did."

Nate's body ached from the night's labor. His palms were blistered, his shirt streaked with soot. At Mrs. Boyle's table, she clucked over him like a hen. "You'll blister yourself into uselessness if you keep at it so hard," she warned, setting down porridge. "Courage is fine, but courage and sense are finer."

Eliza, pale with fatigue but steady in her breath, smiled softly. "He saved more than timbers," she said. "He saved neighbors."

Jazz Corcoran, tuning his fiddle nearby, wagged a bow. "Saved my fiddle too—the flames near licked it when I wasn't looking. I owe you a tune, Harper."

A Town Rebuilding

By afternoon, Tombstone had nearly resumed its rhythm. Carpenters measured damages, children collected blackened nails, merchants argued over losses and debts. Nate joined a crew clearing rubble, his strength earning him nods from men who'd once seen him as just another drifter.

At the Epitaph, Eliza worked beside Clara Finch and Amos Dake. The editor's pen scratched with fire of its own, praising "neighbors who formed a bucket line as stout as any regiment." Clara tucked Eliza's latest column into the corner: Hands passed water hand to hand until they felt like family.

"You've a knack for saying what's true," Clara said, pressing her spectacles up her nose. "Plain words suit a rough town. Keep writing."

Ground for Hope

That evening, when the heat loosened its grip, Nate and Eliza walked along Fremont, then turned north where the street thinned. The air carried the scent of smoke and something cleaner beneath it—new beginnings. Nate stopped beside a vacant lot edged with scrub, the kind of ground a man might one day build on.

"Kittredge says the Grand Central's steady work for months," he said. "And the hardware man's keeping me busy besides. I was thinking—if we set a foundation here, we might make a home."

Eliza studied the ground, then the sky above it—wide, forgiving, endless. "A porch to catch the morning light," she said softly. "A place to breathe without counting steps."

Nate smiled. "A place for you to write, and for me to hammer without Mrs. Boyle complaining I'm waking her guests."

The image lingered between them—a hope framed in dust and possibility.

Whispers Below

That night, a miner at the boarding house spoke low over his stew. "The pumps can't keep pace," he said. "Water's rising down deep. If it floods, men'll be out of work and in the street."

Nate frowned, remembering the tremor of timbers under weight, the drip of the earth's secret breath. Eliza laid her hand over his. "Then we'll pray the timbers hold," she said quietly. But in her notebook that night she wrote: The town's enemies aren't always fire or men with bottles. Sometimes it is the earth itself, testing whether we belong.

The Night's Quiet

Later, lying in their narrow bed, they listened to the silence after so much clamor. For the first time since arriving, Eliza felt cautious hope—neighbors had shown their mettle, and she and Nate had been part of it.

But beneath that quiet, she fancied she heard a distant sound: pumps beating under stone, keeping Tombstone alive as surely as lungs kept her alive.

Chapter 9
River Under Stone

Below the Surface

The morning sun threw long shadows across Allen Street as Nate met Silas P. Kittredge at the Grand Central shaft. The engineer adjusted his spectacles and motioned him toward the cage.

"You've set braces well enough, Harper," he said. "Time you saw what we're fighting."

The cage rattled downward like loose teeth. The air grew damp; the drip of unseen water echoed through the dark. At the lowest level, the gallery widened into a cavern where pumps labored, rods thudding like the heartbeat of some buried beast. Water gleamed black at the edges, never still, always rising.

"This is the river under our feet," Kittredge said. "The pumps hold it back, but they never rest. If they fail—" He stopped. The hiss and churn spoke the rest.

Nate studied the wet timbers, their bases slick with seepage. He felt the weight of mountain above and the pressure of water below—caught between two hungers. "How long can they keep it back?"

Kittredge's mouth thinned. "As long as men feed coal to boilers and pray iron doesn't tire."

Breath and Words

Aboveground, Eliza's strength returned by slow degrees. Each morning she walked beyond Fremont, the desert opening before her like a clean page. She wrote as she went: The mountains breathe slower than men, but their patience lends us ours.

Dr. Avery found her one afternoon and smiled at the sight. "Keep walking, Mrs. Harper. Let your lungs be greedy—there's air enough here to spare."

Her small column in the Epitaph, Notes on the Sunrise Walk, began to draw notice. Men quoted her words at the bar, and Amos Dake grinned to hear it. "Imagine that—a town that drinks whiskey at breakfast and still finds room for poetry."

"People like to see their mornings reflected," Clara said. "She gives them that."

The Water Rises

That evening, Eliza waited on the boardwalk as the sun bled over the hills. Nate emerged from the mine later than usual, clothes damp, face drawn.

"The pumps are working harder," he told her. "Kittredge says we'll hold, but he doesn't sound sure."

She slipped her hand into his. "Then we'll hold too," she said simply. "If the town fights the water, we fight with it."

They walked beneath a sky pricked with stars. The air smelled faintly of coal and sage. For every breath Eliza drew, Nate heard again the steady thud of pistons far below—like a heart too weary to stop.

That night, as they lay awake, the faint pulse of the pumps seemed to travel through the earth into their small room. Nate listened to it like a carpenter listens to the creak of a beam.

“Think it’ll hold?” Eliza whispered.

“It has to,” he said.

Outside, the wind turned cool, whispering across Tombstone’s rooftops. Inside, Eliza reached for her notebook and wrote: Beneath every house, the earth keeps its own clock. And under this town, it beats like a heart that refuses to drown.

She set the book aside, her breathing even and sure, unaware that far below, one of the pumps had begun to groan in protest.

Chapter 10
The Fever

The Heat Descends

The August sun bore down like a blacksmith's hammer. Heat shimmered over Allen Street, turning dust into gold haze. Inside Mrs. Boyle's boarding house, curtains hung still, and even the flies grew languid. Eliza moved slowly through her proofreading, her head heavy, her breath uneven.

By late afternoon Clara Finch frowned across the Epitaph's desk. "You're pale as paper," she said. "Go home before Dake mistakes you for copy and sets you in type."

Eliza tried to laugh, but the sound caught in her throat. She rose, steadying herself against the table. "Just the heat," she murmured, though her steps faltered and her hand pressed tight to her chest.

The Doctor's Verdict

Nate found her in their small room, cheeks flushed, hair damp. "It's nothing," she whispered, but her breath rasped. He laid a hand to her brow—fire under skin. Panic surged.

"I'll fetch Dr. Avery," he said, already reaching for his boots.

Within the hour the doctor arrived, spectacles slipping, bag in hand. He checked her pulse and shook his head. "Fever," he said simply. "Common here, but dangerous for her lungs."

He mixed a draught, cool and bitter, and handed it to Nate. "Keep her cool. Quiet. Her lungs will decide the rest."

A House in Vigil

The boarding house gathered around her. Maggie O'Rourke brought broth; Jazz Corcoran played soft reels in the hall; even stern Mrs. Boyle read scripture in a trembling voice.

Nate moved like a man half-dreaming, changing cloths, coaxing sips of water, whispering encouragement though he wasn't sure she heard. Each cough seemed to tear him open.

On the third night he sat beside her long after others slept. The fever burned bright, her breath rattled shallow, and fear clutched him hard. He took her hand and whispered, "I brought you here to heal. Don't leave me with only dust."

The Light Returns

Toward dawn, Eliza stirred. Her eyes opened, fever-bright. "Write," she breathed.

Nate bent close. "Write what, Liza?"

"Write... about the light." Her fingers reached for the notebook. He placed the pencil between them. With a wavering hand, she traced: The dawn is patient. It waits until we rise to see it.

The pencil slipped from her grasp, and she fell into uneasy sleep. Nate held the book as though it contained her very breath.

Holding On

By the fourth day, the fever burned lower. Dr. Avery examined her and nodded once. “She’s fighting,” he said. “You must match her patience.”

That evening Maggie brought broth and found Nate slumped in the chair. “You’re no use if you fall over,” she said, taking his place. She hummed softly while spooning broth to Eliza’s lips.

When Nate asked about the tune, she said, “Irish lullaby. My mother sang it when fevers came. Some things carry better than medicine.”

Night Watch

Nate lay awake on the cot in the corner, counting her breaths. Each rise and fall was victory. He thought of the pumps below Tombstone, straining against the dark river under stone.

The town fought to breathe—and so did she. He prayed that both would hold.

Chapter 11
The Long Afternoon

Breaking the Heat

The fever broke with the dawn. Nate woke in his chair to find Eliza breathing easier, her skin cool and damp. For a long moment he only stared, scarcely daring to move. Then he called out, and Mrs. Boyle hurried in, apron askew, followed by Dr. Avery.

"She's through the worst," the doctor said after a long listen at her chest. "Feed her light, keep her quiet. Her body remembers how to live."

Nate nearly wept with relief. Mrs. Boyle merely barked, "Fetch water, Mr. Harper. And scrape that soot off your face before you frighten the patient."

Slow Recovery

For two days Eliza drifted between sleep and waking, her voice weak but her eyes brightening. Neighbors cycled through—bread, broth, desert flowers. Jazz Corcoran stood in the hall, drawing tender notes from his fiddle as if music itself could mend what fever had frayed.

One afternoon Maggie lingered after bringing tea. Eliza, pale but curious, asked softly, "Do you have family here?"

The dressmaker hesitated. "Had a husband once. Came west chasing silver, found whiskey instead. Buried him at Boothill two years past. The town gave me work, and I stitched myself back together."

Eliza reached for her hand. "Then you know what it is to lean on neighbors."

Maggie smiled faintly. "Aye. And you'll find Tombstone leans back—for all its noise."

Light and Ink

By week's end Eliza could sit by the window, notebook on her lap. Between rests she scribbled: Neighbors bring bowls and songs as though each were medicine. A rough town, softened by kindness.

Clara Finch arrived with a bundle of proofs. "Your column can wait," she said briskly, though her voice wavered. "Still, when you're ready, we'll print a line or two about light breaking through fever. People like to be reminded mornings return."

The Work Resumes

Nate returned to the Grand Central. The weight of stone seemed heavier, yet he swung the mallet with new resolve. Each timber he set felt like a promise—that he would build more than braces in the dark; he would build a life in the sun.

When he came home, Eliza waited in her chair, smiling. "I listened for your step all afternoon," she said.

"And I thought of you with every strike," he answered. "Kept my arm honest."

A New Foundation

One long afternoon, sunlight spilling across the floor, Eliza laid aside her notebook. “Nate,” she said softly, “we’ve borrowed this room long enough. Don’t you think it’s time to set our own walls?”

He looked at her, startled. “I was waiting until you were stronger.”

“I’m strong enough to want a home,” she said, steady as breath.

Nate nodded slowly. “Then we’ll find the land. Build before the season turns.”

Eliza smiled. The fever had taken her strength but left her will sharpened like sunlight after rain. They would not merely survive Tombstone—they would belong to it.

Chapter 12
Foundations

The Claim

The September sun leaned gentler as Nate walked the edge of town with Silas P. Kittredge. The engineer pointed with his stick toward a stretch of land just north of Fremont, where the mesquite thinned and the ground rose firm.

"Not much to look at," he said, "but it drains well. Yours if you stake it—few dollars and a promise to build before winter."

Nate planted his boots in the dust, feeling its steadiness. He pictured walls rising, a roof catching morning light. "I'll take it," he said simply.

That evening, over stew, he set the deed before Eliza. Her eyes widened. "Nate, you've gone and bought us a home."

"Not yet," he said. "But I'll build it. My hands know how."

Raising Beams

Within a week he was hauling timbers with a borrowed wagon, marking the lines with string. The first swing of his hammer rang like a promise.

Men from the boarding house came to lend shoulders. Maggie O'Rourke brought a jug of lemonade and stitched beneath the shade. Jazz Corcoran fiddled a tune of encouragement and mischief.

Even Mrs. Boyle appeared one afternoon, hands on hips. "A house of your own means no more stew on my table," she said. "I'll forgive you, provided I'm invited for the first meal you burn."

Eliza laughed from her stool, sketching rafters in her notebook. Foundations are promises, she wrote. Wood set into earth to say: we intend to stay.

Words and Wood

One evening Clara Finch came straight from the Epitaph, still ink-stained. She walked the rising frame, assessing the joinery.

"Straight lines," she said. "Good work. Better than most sentences."

Nate grinned. "Words may last longer than wood."

"Only if someone sets them true," Clara answered, offering Eliza a rare smile. "Between your columns and his hammer, you may leave something worth remembering."

Sky Through the Rafters

As days passed, the frame climbed higher. Nate worked until his arms trembled, then worked more. At night he returned with splinters in his palms, and Eliza kissed each one as if it were a medal.

When the first rafters met, they walked to the plot together. The half-built skeleton stood open to the stars.

"This is where we'll be," Nate said softly. "Through whatever storms come."

Eliza leaned against him. "Then let them come," she murmured. "We'll answer with walls and a roof."

The Letter

But the world beyond their little town was not done with them. One afternoon a stagecoach from the east rattled into Tombstone, trailing dust and Ohio memories. At supper, Mrs. Boyle laid a letter beside Eliza's plate.

The envelope bore her mother's careful hand. Eliza stared at it as if it might sing or sting. Nate's gaze met hers across the table. Both knew what such a letter might carry.

Chapter 13
The Letter from Ohio

The Opening

The envelope sat on the table like a stone. Eliza traced her mother's looping script before breaking the seal.

My dearest daughter, the letter began. Your father and I pray the air has done you good, yet each day without word weighs heavy. Ohio may be damp, but it is home. We beg you return before winter claims you. Our house is empty without your laughter.

When she reached the closing—Come home, before it is too late—Eliza folded the page and pressed it to her lips.

Mrs. Boyle cleared her throat. "Homesick mothers write strong letters. Don't mistake longing for command."

Eliza's eyes glistened. "She fears I'll fade here."

Nate leaned forward. "What do you believe, Liza?"

She looked toward the half-built frame visible through the window. "That the desert has given me breath," she said quietly. "But her words make me doubt."

The Pull of Home

The next days carried an undercurrent of restlessness. Eliza worked at the Epitaph, her pencil steady but her thoughts eastward. Clara noticed.

"Letters from home are like mirrors," she said. "They show who you were, not always who you are."

Nate threw himself at the build, hammering until his shoulders ached. Each swing was an argument against leaving. But some evenings, when he looked up, he caught Eliza reading her mother's words by lamplight, her face unreadable.

The Choice

One twilight they walked the edge of town. The Dragoon Mountains glowed violet against the sky. Nate broke the silence.

"If you wish to go back, we'll go," he said. "I won't keep you where your heart won't rest."

Eliza turned, startled. "And leave the house you've built? The neighbors who've held us? The air that lets me breathe?" She shook her head. "No, Nate. But I must answer her truthfully."

The Reply

Back at the boarding house, she sat with a fresh sheet of paper. Her hand trembled at first, then steadied.

Mother, she wrote, the desert is fierce, yet it has given me strength Ohio could not. I cough less, I walk farther, I laugh more. Nate has good work, and we are building a home. Your longing pulls me, but my heart is here. Please believe I am not lost—only rooted in new soil.

When she sealed the envelope, she handed it to Nate. “Will you post it?”

He kissed her forehead. “With pride.”

The Quiet After

That night, as the lamplight dimmed, Eliza whispered, “I chose the desert today.”

Nate drew her close. “Then the desert chose us, too.”

Outside, the frame of their house stood silver in the moonlight—a promise waiting for walls, and a life waiting to be lived.

Chapter 14
Timbers and Promises

A Visit from the Press

The letter to Ohio was scarcely on its way when Tombstone's crossroads tested the Harpers again. One blazing afternoon, Nate stood at the rising frame of their house, hammer in hand, when Clara Finch appeared, her boots powdered in dust and her expression set for truth.

"Word is your wife's family wants her back east," she said without ceremony. "But I saw her at the Epitaph this morning—breathing easy, steady as a clock. That's not Ohio in her chest. That's Tombstone."

Nate rested the hammer across his palm. "She chose to stay," he said quietly. "But choice doesn't stop doubt from sneaking in."

Clara's sharp eyes softened. "Then build that house high enough she can see past doubt," she said. "And don't think you're raising it alone."

The Town Lends Its Hands

True to her word, the town gathered. Jazz Corcoran brought a pair of idle miners and his fiddle, turning the lifting of beams into a dance. Maggie O'Rourke stitched curtains from scraps of calico, holding them up like banners of defiance. Even Deputy Frank Valdez arrived in shirtsleeves, lending quiet muscle to the heaviest timbers.

Mrs. Boyle came last, carrying a basket of biscuits that could have shamed a baker. “A boarding-house keeper knows when her chicks are ready for their own roost,” she said. “But you’ll have me to dinner once a month or I’ll consider this betrayal.”

Eliza watched from a chair in the shade, cheeks pink with pride. Each swing of the hammer, each laugh through the dust, was a chorus declaring the Harpers belonged. She wrote a line in her notebook: A town that builds together forgives the wind.

Raising the Frame

As the sun dropped low, Nate stood on the half-laid floor, surveying what they had built. The scent of fresh pine filled the air. “Here we are, Liza,” he said. “No turning back now.”

She slipped her arm through his. “I don’t want to turn back. Ohio is memory. This—” she gestured to the open rafters glowing gold in sunset—“this is breath and tomorrow.”

From Allen Street came the thunder of hooves. The stage rattled past, the driver cracking his whip and calling, “Benson! Tucson! All points east!”

Eliza’s eyes followed the dust cloud until it faded into the horizon. She exhaled slowly. “The world will always call,” she murmured. “But I’ve chosen where to answer.”

The House-Raising Supper

That evening the boarding house filled with laughter.

Mrs. Boyle permitted music, Maggie poured cider, and Jazz sawed lively tunes until the windows shook.

Amos Dake arrived, ink still fresh on his cuffs. "To foundations," he toasted. "In print or in pine—they hold more than they seem."

Eliza lifted her cup. "And to the neighbors who help us set them."

Glasses clinked, voices rose, and even Mrs. Boyle smiled—briefly, as if it were against her better judgment.

Crossroads

Later, in the hush of their small room, Eliza leaned against Nate's shoulder. "Did you see them?" she said softly. "All working together, laughing like kin? Tombstone isn't just a place—it's people binding each other's lives."

Nate brushed a hand through her hair. "Then we're bound, Liza. Crossroads or not, this is the road we're meant to follow."

Outside, the night hummed with the life of Allen and Fremont—the laughter from saloons, the rattle of wagon wheels, the hammering that never quite stopped. And above it all, their house frame stood tall in the moonlight, a promise made of wood, sweat, and stubborn hope.

Chapter 15
Storm over the Desert

The Warning

The house rose quickly in the crisp October air. Rafters reached skyward, walls squared true, and Nate's hammer rang from dawn till dusk. Each strike felt like a vow—that he and Eliza would not be driven from Tombstone. Neighbors came and went, lending tools, advice, and gossip in equal measure.

But the desert, generous in breath, was merciless in temper. One afternoon the wind shifted hard from the south, hot and full of grit. By evening the sky had turned to copper. Deputy Valdez, passing by, shaded his eyes toward the roofline.

"Storm coming," he called. "Tie her down tight."

Nate looked at the half-laid rafters, jaw set. "We'll weather it."

Valdez shook his head. "The desert doesn't care what men promise—only what they prepare."

The Tempest

The storm broke like a cavalry charge. Wind screamed through the mesquite, driving dust before it in waves. The Harpers huddled in Mrs. Boyle's parlor with the other boarders as shutters banged and lanterns guttered. Jazz Corcoran tried to coax a tune from his fiddle to drown the howling, but his bow quivered against the strings.

Eliza sat rigid, clutching Nate's hand. "The house—" she began.

"We built her square," he said, though worry flickered in his eyes. "She'll stand."

Mrs. Boyle sniffed. "Hope's a fine material, but nails are finer. We'll see which you used more."

After the Fury

When the storm finally staggered off toward the Dragoons, the night lay still and scraped bare. The Harpers stepped outside, coughing on the dust that coated every board and window. Fences leaned drunkenly. Wagons stood half-buried. Tombstone looked as if the desert had tried to reclaim it in a single breath.

They hurried to the edge of town where their new house stood—or what might remain of it.

By lamplight they saw rafters tilted, shingles scattered like playing cards. The frame groaned but stood its ground. Nate pressed his hand against a beam and felt it tremble under the storm's memory.

"She's still breathing," he whispered.

Eliza slipped her arm through his. "So are we."

Neighbors in the Night

Lanterns bobbed along Allen Street as neighbors appeared one by one. Maggie O'Rourke arrived with a coil of rope. "Tie her down before the next gust gets ideas," she ordered.

Jazz fetched nails from his kit; Valdez set his shoulder to a leaning post. Even Amos Dake, fresh from the Epitaph, brought spare boards. “Ink won’t hold this town together,” he said, “but I’ve got a hammer that might.”

Under the lantern glow, they worked side by side, bracing timbers, straightening beams, and driving nails with the stubborn rhythm of defiance. The storm had scattered them for hours; rebuilding gathered them again.

Morning Light

By dawn, the house stood battered but unbroken. The air smelled of wet dust and new resolve. Nate slumped in the doorway, too weary to move. Eliza leaned beside him, her hair streaked with grit but her eyes shining clear.

“This place,” she said softly, “tries us again and again. Yet every trial binds us closer—to the house, to our neighbors, to each other.”

Nate brushed the dust from her cheek. “Then let the storms come,” he said. “We’ll build stronger each time.”

Behind them, the first rays of sun slipped through the ragged rafters, painting the floor in stripes of gold. To Eliza, it looked like a promise written in light.

Chapter 16
The House Breathes

Rebuilding Resolve

In the weeks after the storm, the Harpers worked with renewed purpose. Every bent rafter was straightened, every loosened joint wedged and nailed. Neighbors drifted in daily—Valdez hauling lumber with quiet strength, Maggie O'Rourke sewing curtains that fluttered like victory flags, Jazz Corcoran fiddling lively reels to keep the hammers in time. The gale had stolen days of labor, but neighbors arrived each dawn until rafters stood true again.

Even Mrs. Boyle, who had sworn she'd never set foot on a construction site, appeared with a basket of sandwiches and her sharpest tongue. "If a man pauses long enough to think, he's already behind," she scolded, handing out food as fiercely as orders.

By November, the house stood whole: walls solid, roof shingled, windows snug against the wind. A brick chimney rose straight and proud, and Nate framed a small porch facing east—exactly as Eliza had dreamed. A rocker waited there, polished smooth and patient for the sunrise.

Neighbors and Celebration

The first evening in their finished home, the Harpers opened their door to everyone who had lifted a hand. The table was a pair of planks laid over sawhorses, the chairs borrowed and mismatched, but laughter filled the rafters more surely than any insulation.

Jazz fiddled in the doorway, children ran shouting through unfinished rooms, and even Clara Finch—perpetually ink-stained and unamused—raised her cup.

“To words and walls both,” she declared. “May they stand.”

Amos Dake grinned. “And may your porch be wide enough for neighbors who never wait for invitations.”

Mrs. Boyle sniffed, eyes glistening. “If you don’t burn the biscuits, I may forgive you for leaving my table.”

Eliza, her cheeks bright with pride, leaned against Nate’s shoulder. “We dreamed of walls,” she said softly, “but you all built them with us.”

Listening to the House

When the last guests had gone and the night fell still, the Harpers sat alone on the porch. The air was cool, scented faintly of sage and smoke. Stars burned above the desert, unblinking and close.

Nate drew his arm around Eliza’s shoulders. “Do you hear it?” he asked.

She tilted her head. “Hear what?”

“The house,” he said. “She’s breathing.”

Eliza listened. The timbers gave small, contented creaks as they settled into the cool. The wind slipped under the eaves with a sigh, and the chimney murmured softly, like a throat clearing before speech. Together it sounded alive—a new creature stretching its frame.

She smiled. “Then she breathes with us. May she breathe long.”

Nate kissed her hair. “She will, Liza. This house will outlast storms, fire, even doubt.”

The Note in the Night

Later, as Nate slept, Eliza opened her notebook by lamplight. Her pen moved slowly, her words steady and sure:

The house breathes with us. Neighbors filled it with laughter before we even swept the floor. It is humble, but it is ours. The desert has tested us and found us willing to stay.

She closed the book and laid it on the windowsill, where the moon turned its cover silver. Outside, the wind curled softly around the eaves like a lullaby.

Beside her, Nate’s breathing deepened into sleep—a rhythm that matched the creak and sigh of the new home settling into its place.

And beyond the walls, the desert stretched wide and silent, its trials spent for now. The house exhaled once, faintly, as though content to stand its watch.

Chapter 17
Dry Air & Good Hope

A Gentle Winter

Winter came softly to Tombstone—air cool but clear, sunlight generous without cruelty. In the Harper house, mornings began with light spilling across the porch, Eliza in her rocker, Nate bent over a beam or chair meant for a neighbor.

The house, as Nate had promised, breathed with them: timbers creaked in the warmth, windows caught each changing hue of sky. The air itself seemed to settle easier inside their walls.

Eliza's strength returned with the season. Each day she walked farther into the desert, notebook in hand, the landscape now as familiar as her own pulse. What had begun as scribbles for herself had become a column readers sought in the Epitaph.

Notes on the Sunrise Walk appeared weekly, her words plain but true—of mesquite that cast playful shade, of skies that poured light instead of rain, of neighbors who carried buckets as though passing trust hand to hand.

Amos Dake grumbled good-naturedly, "She's made poets out of miners."

Clara Finch merely nodded, which in Clara's language was the highest possible praise.

The Heart of the Town

The Harpers' home soon became a gathering place. Maggie O'Rourke hung curtains of calico roses; Jazz Corcoran played on the porch until stars scattered like applause. Deputy Valdez claimed the rocker opposite Eliza, content to rest in silence after long patrols.

Even Mrs. Boyle conceded, over Sunday supper, "You've built a house that doesn't just hold people—it invites them."

One evening the town itself seemed to agree. A group of miners passing along Allen Street tipped their hats toward the little house.

"That's Harper's place," one said. "Solid fellow—pulled McGinnis from the shaft, stood through the fire. And his wife—she writes the mornings better than the sun does."

Eliza overheard from the porch. Her chest tightened, not with illness but with a swelling pride that filled her like air after rain.

Christmas Eve

By December the house gleamed warm with life. On Christmas Eve, the Harpers hosted a small gathering. Neighbors filled the rooms—boots scuffed the floor, laughter tangled with the scent of stew and pine.

Jazz fiddled Silent Night until the chatter softened, and voices joined the tune, uneven but heartfelt. Eliza stood near the window, candlelight trembling on her face. Nate took her hand.

"Do you remember our first night here?" he whispered. "The dust in our lungs, the noise outside, how we wondered if we'd made a mistake?"

Eliza smiled. "I remember. And I remember thinking I might not see another winter. But the desert gave me breath—and you gave me courage."

"And you," Nate said, his voice low, "gave me reason to build."

The Last Entry

When the guests were gone and the quiet returned, Eliza opened her notebook by lamplight for the last entry of the year. Her handwriting flowed easily now, confident as her breath.

We came west for air—and found it, and more besides. We found neighbors who stand as kin, a town that tests but also shelters, and a home that breathes with us. Tombstone is no easy place, but it is ours. In its dry air, we have found good hope.

She set down her pencil and smiled at the page.

Outside, the desert stretched wide and waiting beneath a quilt of stars. Nate joined her on the porch, his arm settling around her shoulders. Together they sat in the hush, the soft exhale of their house blending with the quiet pulse of the land.

The home stood steady against the cool wind, alive with its own breath—a small, stubborn proof that hope could take root even in dry ground.

And together, at last, the Harpers were settled.

The End

Also in the Arizona Dust series

Coming soon from Edith Clairmont

Good Hope Rising
Nate and Eliza Harper's story continues as hope takes deeper root in Tombstone, and the promises they've built begin to face the weight of real life.

What the Body Keeps
Deputy Frank Valdez and Dr. Avery take center stage in a thoughtful Tombstone mystery where truth, memory, and quiet danger refuse to stay buried.

www.ingramcontent.com/pod-product-compliance
Lightning Source LLC
LaVergne TN
LVHW020049110826
845155LV00029B/704